The William Shakespeare

CHILDREN'S COLLECTION

Dados Internacionais de Catalogação na Publicação (CIP) de acordo com ISBD

S5271m Shakespeare, William
Much ado about nothing / William Shakespeare. - Jandira, SP : W. Books, 2025.
96 p. ; 12,80cm x 19,80cm. - (Classics).

ISBN: 978-65-5294-202-9

1. Literatura inglesa. 2. Clássicos. 3. Aventura. 4. Fantasia. 5. Imaginação. I. Título.
II. Série.

2025-2511 CDD 823
CDU 821.111

Elaborada por Lucio Feitosa - CRB-8/8803
Índice para catálogo sistemático:
1. Literatura inglesa 823
2. Literatura inglesa 821.111-3

The William Shakespeare Children's Collection

Text based on the original play by William Shakespeare,
adapted by Gemma Barder
Illustrations by Mai Ngo

1st edition in 2025
www.cirandacultural.com.br

EASY CLASSICS

William Shakespeare

Much Ado About Nothing

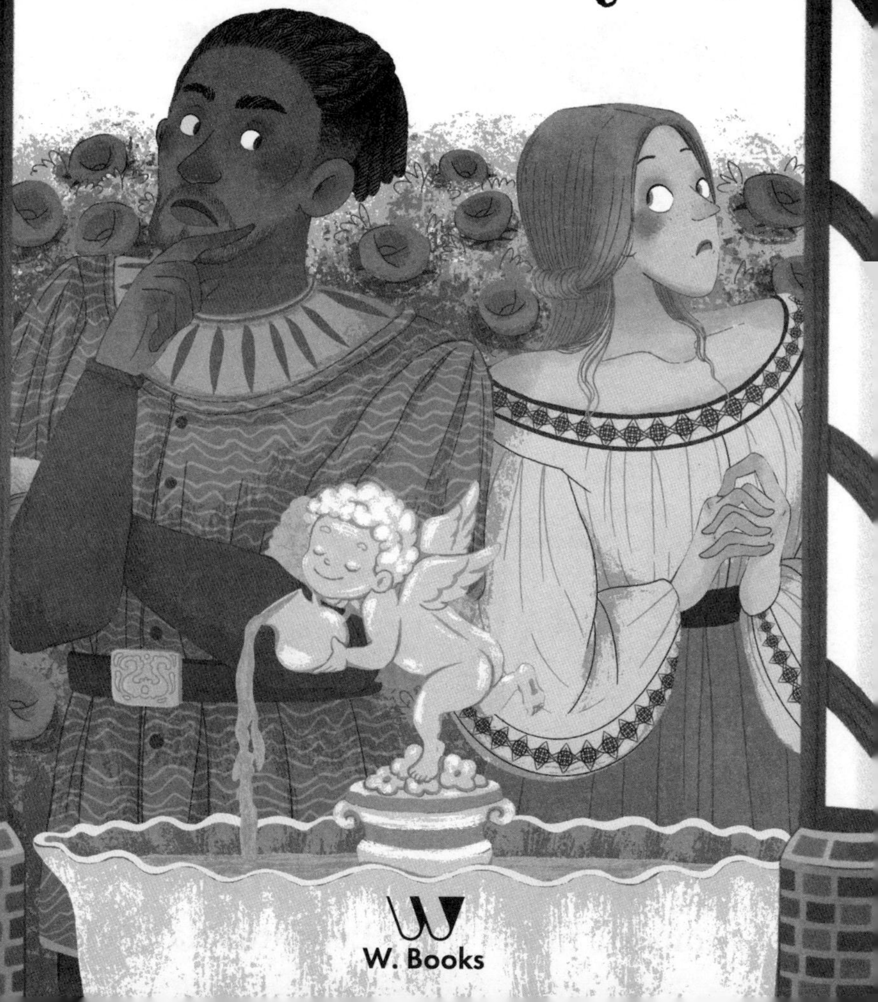

W. Books

Leonato

Governor of Messina

Don Pedro

Prince of Arragon

Benedick

A lord from Padua

Claudio

A lord from Florence

Beatrice

Leonato's niece

Hero

Leonato's daughter

Don John

Don Pedro's half-brother

Borachio

Don John's follower

Dogberry

Constable in charge of the watch

Friar Francis

Member of the church

Chapter One

Hero and her cousin Beatrice were waiting at the castle's port, staring at the small ship on the horizon. It was heading towards them and their city of Messina.

'I don't know why *he* has to come back here,' said Beatrice as the ship got closer and closer.

'If you are talking about Benedick,

horizon

The line where the Earth and the sky appear to meet.

then it is because he is part of Don Pedro's army,' said Hero. 'And is his father's oldest friend.'

Beatrice folded her arms as a messenger appeared and was greeted by Hero's father, Leonato.

'Don Pedro and his soldiers are just behind me,' said the messenger.

'I was sent on ahead to make sure you are expecting them.'

'You are all welcome,' said Leonato. 'We have rooms for everyone in the castle.'

'You are most kind, Leonato,' said Don Pedro, appearing behind the messenger. 'Let me introduce you to my brave men. Of course, you already know Benedick.'

Benedick stepped forwards and bowed gracefully. He glanced at Beatrice who rolled her eyes in annoyance.

'Now, let me introduce you to Claudio,' said Don Pedro as a young soldier removed his hat and bowed. Claudio turned to Beatrice and Hero and bowed again, catching Hero's eye.

'And finally, this is my brother, Don John.'

'Half-brother,' Don John corrected. He was tall with a thin moustache and a scowl on his face.

As Don John stepped away, Don Pedro sighed. 'Forgive his rudeness,' Don Pedro said. 'In truth, he was fighting against us, and when his army was defeated he promised to join us. But I fear he is not happy about it.'

Leonato looked at Don John with suspicion. Eventually, he said: 'Don Pedro, any relative of yours will be treated as one of the family while you stay with us. Now come! Let my servants help you to unload the ship.'

As the two friends stepped away from the crowd, Claudio

nervously approached Hero and Beatrice.

'It is a pleasure to meet you both,' he said, politely. 'Miss Hero, you look very much like your father ... that is ... a prettier version of course!'

As Claudio blushed, Benedick threw a playful arm around his shoulder.

'Forgive my

friend, ladies,' he said. 'He is not as confident as I am.'

'Confident or arrogant?' snapped Beatrice.

Hero rolled her eyes and sighed.

'You will get used to their bickering, Claudio,' said Hero. 'My cousin and Benedick have not said a kind word to each other since the day they met.'

Beatrice laughed. 'Kind? I'm not sure Benedick knows the meaning of such a *long* word.'

arrogant

Someone who acts like they are more important than others.

Benedick put his hands on his hips in frustration. 'Why, more than anyone else in the whole of Italy, do you annoy me so much?'

Beatrice smirked.

'I'm just talented, I suppose,' she said, before walking

away, leaving Benedick seething.

Hero and Claudio glanced at each other, each one smiling at the behaviour of their friends.

'Listen, everyone, if you please!' Leonato interrupted in a loud voice. 'To celebrate the victory of my good friend Don Pedro and his army, there will be a grand masquerade ball tonight!'

masquerade

A type of party at which the guests wear masks that cover their faces.

A ripple of excitement spread amongst the soldiers. All but one was pleased. All but Don John.

Later that day, as the soldiers settled into the castle and preparations were busily underway for the ball, Benedick found Claudio alone in the gardens. Claudio had a piece of paper and a feather quill in his hand.

quill

A pen made from the hollow stem of a feather.

‘Whatever are you doing?’ asked Benedick.

Claudio jumped and tried to hide the paper from his friend.

‘Nothing …’ he replied.

Benedick grinned.

'Well … if you must know, I am writing a poem,' Claudio replied.

'A poem for who?' asked Benedick. Claudio handed the paper to him. He scanned the words before realising. 'Hero? Are you in love with Hero?'

'Shhh!' said Claudio, worried that someone would overhear them. 'Yes, I think I am – from the moment I saw her at the port. How could anyone not be in love with her beauty and charm?'

Benedick thought for a moment.

'Well, I suppose she is pretty enough,' he said. 'Of course, she is not as pretty as her cousin. It is a shame Beatrice is so annoying, otherwise she would be perfect.'

'There you both are!' said Don Pedro, striding towards them. 'I have masks for both of you for tonight's ball … Whatever is the matter with you, Claudio?'

Before Claudio could answer, Benedick jumped in, cheekily.

'He is in love with Hero, sir,' he said. 'But he's too shy to talk to her.'

Claudio blushed.

'Oh, my dear boy!' said Don Pedro, kindly. 'Well, I do think Hero is lovely, but I understand how hard it is to talk to someone about how you feel.'

Don Pedro's eyes flashed with joy. It was the same look he got when he was working out a tricky military manoeuvre.

'That's it! Everyone will be wearing masks tonight,' he began.

'So, *I* will dance with Hero and pretend to be you. I'll tell her how you feel about her and we will see if she feels the same way about you!'

The plan was set. Now all they had to do was wait for the ball to begin.

Chapter Two

Borachio finally found Don John lurking in a dark corner of the castle. Borachio was one of the few soldiers who liked Don John and was desperate for his attention. Now, at last, he had something that might make Don John take notice.

'I … have just … heard … something … in the garden … about your brother,' he panted.

'What is it?' asked Don John,

impatiently. He was fiddling with his mask, determined not to attend the ball.

Borachio proceeded to tell Don John about Don Pedro's plan to help Claudio confess his love for Hero. As he spoke, a small, satisfied smile spread across Don John's face.

'This is certainly something I would like to know more about, Borachio. In fact, it's given me a rather good idea,' he said. 'And do you know the best

part? It means I get revenge on my "heroic" brother and his best soldier, too. If I can cross him any way, I bless myself every way.'

The ball was a grand affair, with tables full of colourful food and music to dance to. Don Pedro soon asked Hero to dance, telling her he was Claudio, as the *real* Claudio watched on.

Benedick smiled as he saw Beatrice standing on her own and decided to play a trick of his own.

He gave himself a false name and asked Beatrice to dance. Beatrice, however, was far too clever for Benedick. Knowing exactly who he was, she accepted.

'So, tell me, what do you make of young Benedick?' asked Benedick.

Beatrice grinned. 'Oh, him?' she replied. 'Nothing much. I've heard they only keep him around to make the other soldiers look good.'

Benedick glared at Beatrice, who simply giggled back, enjoying her joke.

As the dance ended, Beatrice curtseyed to Benedick and winked at him from behind her mask. Frustrated that Beatrice had not been fooled by him, Benedick stormed off.

Meanwhile, as Claudio watched Don Pedro and Hero take to the floor for a second dance,

he was joined in his hiding spot by Don John.

'Oh, she is pretty, isn't she?' said Don John, following Claudio's gaze to the dancing couple. 'I'm sure my brother is all set to propose to her soon.'

'What?' asked Claudio, alarmed, knowing this couldn't be true.

'Oh yes, don't you know? Don Pedro is madly in love with Hero and wants to marry her. That is why they are dancing at this very moment!' Don John grinned as he saw his lie take effect.

Claudio's face fell. He thought Don Pedro was helping him, but all along he wanted Hero for himself?

Happy that his work was done, Don John drifted into the crowd, leaving a devastated Claudio alone.

Then Benedick appeared, eager to hear if their plan had worked. He was shocked to see Claudio's sad face.

'Oh, my friend, does Hero not feel the same about you?' he asked.

'I would not know,' said Claudio. 'Don Pedro wants Hero for himself!'

Before Benedick could ask anything else, Claudio ran away through the crowds of happy dancing guests.

As the evening wore on, Benedick watched as Beatrice danced with different soldiers.

A growing feeling of jealously bubbled in his stomach. Although he did not want to admit it, he liked Beatrice.

'Benedick! Where is Claudio? I have been looking for him everywhere,' said Don Pedro. 'Who are you staring at so intently?'

Benedick tore his eyes away from Beatrice. 'No one!' he lied. 'And Claudio left when he found out you

had fallen in love with Hero.'

Don Pedro laughed at this silly claim.

'Me?' he said. 'I am not in love with Hero! Who would think such a ridiculous thing? She admitted to me that she loves Claudio!'

Finally, Benedick found Claudio and, as the last of the guests stumbled off to their beds, Don Pedro explained everything. Claudio felt a wave of relief flood through him, as well as feeling a little foolish that he had been so easily tricked by Don John.

'I have spoken to Leonato,' said

Don Pedro. 'And we agree that the wedding should take place as soon as possible while we are all together at the castle.'

Benedick congratulated Claudio, and their friends all clapped and cheered.

Chapter Three

A few days later, preparations for Hero and Claudio's wedding were in full swing. As Hero and her maid Ursula were making flower garlands, they were joined by Don Pedro and Claudio.

'Ladies, I have a question for you,' said Don Pedro, sitting down to join them. 'I believe that

Benedick is in love with Beatrice and I wondered if Beatrice felt the same?'

Hero smiled.

'Of course she does!' she said. 'Although she would deny it if you asked her. And so would he!'

'Then it is up to us to show them that they are perfect for each other,' said Don Pedro.

With the plan agreed, Don Pedro and Claudio walked through the gardens until they spotted Benedick sitting alone in the sunshine. Quietly, they positioned themselves behind a bush, just far enough away from Benedick so that they could be overheard. With a wink to each other, they began the first stage of their plan.

'Are you *sure*, Claudio? I mean, I always thought Beatrice hated Benedick,' said Don Pedro in a loud voice.

At the mention of his name,

Benedick jumped up and listened carefully.

‘Oh no!’ replied Claudio, trying not to laugh. ‘Beatrice is head over heels in love with Benedick. If only he knew!’

As Claudio and Don Pedro walked away, a stunned but delighted Benedick sat down heavily on the wooden garden bench, snapping it. Hardly realising, he lay among the broken pieces, staring at the bright blue sky above him. He felt overjoyed. Beatrice loved him and he loved her! He closed his eyes and felt the warm sun cover him. It was only

when he felt a shadow sheltering his face that he broke out of his daydream.

'What on earth are you doing?' asked Beatrice, standing over him. 'For some reason, I have been asked to come and find you and tell you that it is time for dinner.'

Benedick scrambled to his feet.

'Why, thank you, Beatrice,' he said.

Beatrice stared at him in disbelief.

There was no sarcastic comment. No witty remark. It was strange, and Beatrice did not like it.

'What is the matter with you?' she asked.

'Nothing, now that you are here,' he replied.

Beatrice rolled her eyes and sighed. She had known Benedick long enough to know that whatever he said probably had some sort of trick behind it.

'Look, come for some food or don't,' she said. 'I really could not care less.'

Benedick grinned as he watched

Beatrice walk away.

Beatrice was still grumbling to herself when she heard whispering in the garden, and her own name mentioned. She stopped.

'That's right, Ursula!' said Hero in a whisper loud enough to be heard by anyone who happened to be passing. 'Benedick is in love with Beatrice!'

'Well, they *are* perfect for each other,' said Ursula, replying in an equally loud whisper. 'But would Beatrice ever let him tell her how he feels – they are always arguing!'

'That is true,' said Hero. 'Maybe one day they will realise what they mean to each other.'

Beatrice was shocked by what she had just heard. Benedick loved her? Could it be true? To her shock, she realised that the thought of Benedick made her happier than she could ever have imagined. The reason she thought about him so much was not because he annoyed her, it was because she was in love with him too!

In another part of the castle, a less romantic plan was being plotted.

Don John was still determined to get revenge on his brother, Don Pedro. He summoned Borachio to his room. His first plan didn't work, so he had a new idea to ruin the happy event that

summon

To bring into existence or readiness.

everyone was looking forward to.

'Borachio, I have a job for you,' said Don John, taking out a small pouch of coins and tossing them to Borachio. 'At 10 p.m, I want you to visit Hero's room when she is not there. Talk to her maid by the window for half an hour, then leave.'

Borachio stared at the coins, then back at Don John.

'Of course, I would be honoured to do

this for you, but why?' he asked.

Don John smiled, wickedly.

'All will become clear, my new friend,' he said. 'Now, on your way.'

Chapter Four

Benedick admired himself in his bedroom mirror. It was the day before Hero and Claudio's wedding, and he wanted to look his best for Beatrice. He was going to speak to her the next time he saw her and tell her that he felt the same.

Meanwhile, Claudio and Don Pedro were going over the last

small details of the ceremony when Don John joined them.

'There you are, brother,' said Don Pedro. 'Where have you been? Are you looking forward to the celebrations tomorrow?'

Don John shook his head slowly.

'I am afraid I have some very bad news,' he said, pretending to be sad. 'Hero is in love with another man.'

Claudio stepped back in anger.

'You have tried to tell me lies

about Hero before, Don John,' he said. 'Why should I believe you this time?'

'I can prove it,' said Don John. 'Meet me in the gardens below Hero's window at 10 p.m this evening and all will be revealed.'

Constable Dogberry had been working for Leonato for many years. His job was to make sure Leonato's castle, lands and family were kept safe. As Leonato was a kind, peace-loving man, there was never much for Dogberry to do, until now … with a wedding.

Leonato was overjoyed that his daughter, Hero, was getting

married to a brave young soldier called Claudio. He wanted to make sure nothing went wrong and, more importantly, that no one ruined the day.

He had instructed Dogberry to make sure there were no strangers in the castle grounds and so, Dogberry had called in his very best officers. Unfortunately for Dogberry, his best officers also happened to be some of the worst policemen in Italy.

'Listen up, men!' said Dogberry. 'Are you good men and true? We have a very important task at hand. The daughter of Leonato is getting married tomorrow and it

is our job to ensure everything goes smoothly. Understand?'

Dogberry looked out at the officers and sighed.

Claudio, Don Pedro and Don John were crouched beside a bush under Hero's window.

'What are we doing here?' Claudio asked, annoyed. 'It is the night before my wedding!'

'Precisely,' said Don John. 'Now, just wait ... yes ... look!'

At that moment, all three of them

looked up as the back of a woman's head appeared at Hero's bedroom window. Although Don John knew it was Hero's maid, he let Claudio and Don Pedro believe it was Hero.

A few moments later, a man

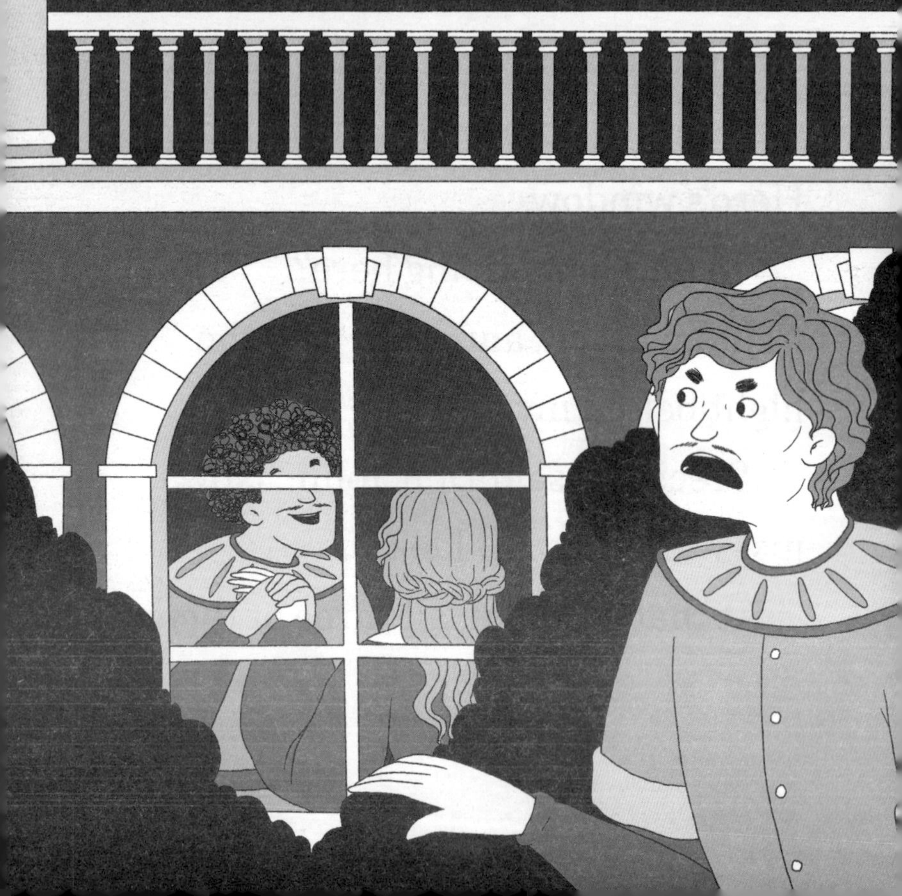

appeared next to her.

'Who is that?' asked Claudio, confused.

'That is the person Hero is *truly* in love with,' lied Don John. 'What are you going to do?'

Claudio's face was red with shock, his eyes filled with angry tears.

'I shall … call off the wedding!' he said, sniffing. 'In front of all our friends and family!'

Don John smiled to himself. His plan had worked.

Later that evening, Dogberry was patrolling the gardens with two of his officers when he saw a man walking towards them out of the darkness. The man was whistling and swinging a pouch of coins in the air. It was Borachio.

'You there!' said Dogberry. 'What business do you have walking the grounds at this late hour?'

Borachio froze. He knew the part he had played in deceiving Claudio would get him into deep trouble.

deceive

Making someone believe something that is not true. Trying to trick or fool a person.

'I ... um ...' Borachio stuttered.

'Men! Seize him!' Dogberry shouted.

Luckily for the officers, Borachio was not hard to catch. He was taken to the castle's jail for questioning.

Chapter Five

Leonato rushed through his castle's grounds to the beautiful chapel. He did not want to be late for his own daughter's wedding. He was so busy, he almost ran straight into his constable.

'Oh, Dogberry, I did not see you there,' he said.

'Sir, I think there is something you ought to kno–' began Dogberry.

‘It will have to wait,’ said Leonato, brushing him off. ‘I am going to be late!’

‘But sir, there was a man in the grounds and …’

Leonato disappeared before Dogberry could say any more.

Outside the chapel, Beatrice was making last minute adjustments to Hero’s veil. She was wearing a beautiful wedding dress,

waiting to marry her one true love.

As soon as Leonato arrived, he took his daughter's arm and walked her down the aisle of the church to meet Claudio who did not look Hero in the eye. Instead, he stared straight ahead at Friar Francis, who began the ceremony.

'Ladies and gentlemen, we

friar

A man who is a member of the Roman Catholic religious order; a monk.

are gathered here today to join together Hero and Clau–'

'No!' screamed Claudio. 'I refuse to marry Hero!'

Hero stared at Claudio in disbelief.

'You are in love with another man!' he cried.

'No!' said Hero. 'It is not true!'

At this moment, Don Pedro stepped forward.

'I am sorry to say that I believe Claudio is telling the truth. We saw you last night, Hero, at your bedroom window,' he said.

Hero looked from face to face in shock.

'It was not me! I love Claudio!

I …' Hero could not speak. Her eyes fluttered and she collapsed to the ground in shock.

Claudio stormed out of the chapel, followed by Don Pedro and a very satisfied-looking Don John.

His plan had finally worked.

Beatrice and Benedick rushed to Hero, helping her to sit up while a shocked Leonato showed the wedding guests out of the chapel.

Friar Francis knelt by Hero's side.

'The poor child,' he said.

'You must not believe what they said about her, Friar Francis,' said Beatrice. 'It is not true!'

'I do not believe it,' he replied, looking kindly at Hero, who was starting to wake.

'Hero has an honest look in her eye. I can always

spot a liar and she is not one. I want to help her, and I believe I know how. We must make Claudio believe that Hero is dead. He will soon regret his actions and realise Hero is innocent.'

Leonato, Benedick and Beatrice all agreed. Leonato and the friar discussed where to hide Hero, while Beatrice approached Benedick.

'Why did you stay and help when Claudio left?' asked Beatrice. 'Is he not your best friend?'

Benedick breathed deeply.

'He is, but …' he paused.

‘I love *you*, Beatrice, and I will do anything to help you.’

Beatrice’s eyes filled with happy tears.

‘I love you too, Benedick.’

Chapter Six

Borachio sat in the castle jail, shivering in the morning light. He had heard the chapel bells ringing for Hero and Claudio's wedding, but he did not know if Don John's plan had worked until Dogberry stormed into his cell.

'Time for you to start answering some questions!' Dogberry demanded. 'Where did you get this money from?'

A young priest was present in

the room to write down the details of Borachio's story.

'A … a friend,' replied Borachio.

'Which friend?' asked Dogberry.

'Don ... Don John,' said Borachio.

‘Bring him here, I am sure he will tell you that I am an honest man and have done nothing wrong.’

At that moment, one of Dogberry's officers arrived with a message. There was much discussion and the young priest looked worried.

‘I’m afraid we cannot bring Don John to save you,’ Dogberry said, slowly. ‘It appears he has run away, and that poor girl, Hero, has died of shock.’

Borachio’s eyes grew wide and he began to tremble.

‘Gone?’ he spluttered. ‘And Hero is dead? Oh, what have I done?’

Borachio began to weep.

Dogberry screwed up the message. He may have been old and perhaps not the best sergeant in Italy, but he had known Hero since she was a child, and the thought that this bumbling man had something to do with her death filled him with rage.

'Stop crying!' he shouted. 'And tell me what you know. The truth! Now!'

Borachio sat back and sniffed.

'I was paid by Don John,'

Borachio began slowly. 'I was to go to Hero's bedroom and stand by the window while I spoke to her maid.'

Dogberry nodded. 'I see,' he replied. 'So, if anyone was watching from outside, they would see a man and woman.'

Borachio nodded, miserably.

'And if that person was Claudio, he would think Hero was in love with someone else, and he would call off the wedding.'

Borachio began to weep again.

'I did not mean for poor Hero to die!' he wailed. 'Please believe me! I will do anything to put things right!'

Dogberry nodded, then fetched the key to unlock Borachio's chains.

'Come with me,' he said. 'There are many people who need to hear your story.'

Chapter Seven

Leonato sat alone in the great hall of his castle. Just a few days before, that same hall had been filled with laughter and dancing. Now, his daughter was in hiding.

Footsteps echoed around the hall as Don Pedro and Claudio approached. Leonato stared at the young man who might have been his son-in-law.

'What do you want?' asked Leonato.

‘We have come to tell you we are leaving,’ said Don Pedro.

‘Good. I do not want to see that boy again,’ said Leonato.

Don Pedro sighed heavily.

'I understand you are upset,' he said. 'But both Claudio and I saw Hero at her bedroom window.'

'It was not her!' Leonato roared, standing up to face the two men. 'And now she has died of shock!'

Claudio stepped back in horror.

'Dead?' he said, his voice trembling. 'Hero has died?'

'Yes, and it is all your fault!'

Before anyone could say another word, Benedick arrived. He glanced at Claudio but stood firmly by Leonato's side.

'Claudio, how could you believe

Hero would love another man?' he asked.

Claudio looked between the faces of the men and struggled to speak.

'We saw … we saw her!' he replied.

'No, you did not,' said a voice. All four men turned to see Dogberry marching towards them with Borachio. Borachio's hands were tied and his face was streaked with tears.

'Tell them what you just admitted to me.' Dogberry pushed Borachio forward.

The sorry man told his story. How Don John had paid him. How it was him standing in the window with Hero's maid – who wasn't aware it was part of his plan – and how Hero was innocent after all.

'Rest assured, sir,' said Dogberry, 'that this man shall be punished for his crimes!'

Leonato held up his hand.

rest assured

Something is definitely the case.
There is no need to worry about it.

'No,' he said. 'Let him go free. Tell him to spread his story far and wide so that everyone knows Hero was innocent.'

When Dogberry had marched Borachio out of the great hall, Claudio fell to his knees.

'Why did I not trust her?' he wailed. 'I killed her! It was me!'

Don Pedro was white with shock.

'We are sorry, old friend,' said Don Pedro. 'Whatever we can do to help you, we will.'

Leonato glanced at Benedick. Of course, the two of them knew that Hero was alive and well, but they had a plan to put into action. A plan to ensure that Claudio and Hero would both be happy.

‘There are two things I want you to do,’ Leonato said. ‘First, you must tell everyone that you were wrong. That my daughter only loved you.’

Claudio nodded through his tears.

'Secondly, you must marry the girl of my choosing tomorrow.'

Although it was a strange request, Claudio did not care.

'I have lost the only person who truly loved me,' he said. 'I will marry whoever you want me to.'

Later that afternoon, Benedick and Beatrice sat in the castle gardens as Benedick told Beatrice everything that had happened that morning.

'If all goes well, there will be a happy ending,' said Benedick.

'Not just for Hero, but for us too!' said Beatrice.

'Well, for you at least,' Benedick teased. 'After all, I am the most handsome man in the city!'

'Perhaps,' replied Beatrice. 'But you are going to marry the most beautiful woman in Italy!'

Chapter Eight

At sunrise the following morning, a tearful Claudio sat alone in the chapel graveyard. The Leonato family tomb stood before him, where he believed his beloved Hero was now at rest.

He held his quill and paper in his hands, much the same as he had done the first morning he had

tomb

A room, usually underground, where bodies are buried.

met Hero. But this time it was not a love poem he was writing, it was a poem to tell anyone who visited the tomb that he was wrong. That Hero was innocent and good and true. When he finished, he placed the poem onto the tomb under a rock, took a deep breath, and went to prepare for his wedding.

Outside the chapel, Hero, Beatrice and their maids were busily getting ready for the wedding. They each had masks to cover their faces. Benedick, Leonato and Friar Francis stood nearby, ready to put their plan into its final stages.

'Quickly!' said Friar Francis. 'I can see Claudio and Don Pedro arriving!'

The ladies all disappeared inside the chapel, ready to begin.

Before Claudio and Don Pedro could reach them, Benedick pulled Leonato to one side. 'I am sorry to tell you this at such a moment,' he began quickly. 'But I am in love with your niece, Beatrice, and wish to marry her with your blessing.'

'Well, thank goodness you two

figured it out in the end!' said Leonato, chuckling. 'Perhaps before the day is over, we will have two happy marriages?'

Benedick smiled but did not answer as Claudio and Don Pedro had joined them at last.

A very sombre-looking Claudio raised his eyes to meet Leonato.

'Where is the lady I am going to marry?' he asked.

'She is inside,' replied Leonato. 'Follow me.'

The men stepped inside the chapel and Claudio took his place next to the masked lady at the altar.

Friar Francis began the ceremony.

'Do you vow to marry whoever is behind this mask?' he asked.

‘I do,’ said Claudio.

At that moment, Hero took off her mask and grinned at Claudio. ‘I do, too!’ she said, throwing her arms around him.

Claudio and Don Pedro were overjoyed that Hero was alive, although a little shocked. Once Claudio had recovered from the surprise, he grasped Hero's hands and begged for the friar to finish the wedding ceremony as quickly as he could.

'Wait!' said Benedick. 'There is one more thing we need to do before the wedding can continue. Friar, have you ever performed a double wedding?'

The friar smiled. 'Well, no, but I am happy to give it a go!' he said. 'Who else wishes to be married this day?'

'Beatrice, if you want to marry me, remove your mask and join me here,' said Benedick, his voice trembling with nerves.

Slowly, Beatrice stepped out from behind Hero and removed her mask.

'Well, I suppose I will,' she said,

teasingly. 'After all, no one else would have you!'

Benedick laughed and twirled Beatrice round in the air.

After the wedding, with Hero and Claudio and Beatrice and Benedick happily married, the celebrations could finally begin.

Don Pedro was just about to help himself to another slice of wedding cake when a messenger burst into the great hall.

'Excuse me, sir,' he said. 'But we thought you would like to know that your

brother, Don John has been captured. We are bringing him back to the castle.'

Don Pedro nodded. 'Thank you,' he said. 'He must pay for the wrong he has done. Will you stay and enjoy the celebrations with us?'

The messenger looked around the room.

'It certainly looks like you are having fun,' said the messenger. 'What has happened here to make so many people happy?'

Don Pedro smiled, looking around the room.

'Oh, much ado about nothing, really,' he laughed.